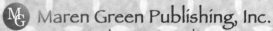 Maren Green Publishing, Inc.

5525 Memorial Avenue North, Suite 6

Oak Park Heights, MN 55082

Toll-free 800-287-1512

Library of Congress Publication-in-data is available.

Text set in Papyrus

Illustrations created digitally

First Edition January 2009

10 9 8 7 6 5 4 3 2 1

Manufactured in China

ISBN 978-1-934277-24-9

www.marengreen.com

Dedicated to our daughters,
Robyn McAllen and Heather McClure.

And also
in grateful appreciation to Midge McGilvray
for being instrumental in getting this book published.

THE DIRTIEST HAIR IN THE WORLD

Written by Bob McAllen

Illustrated by Tom McClure

Our Claire, we hope,
Will soon use soap
Upon her auburn curls

For Mom has seen
Her hair's unclean
Unlike the other girls.

But Claire says, "Phoo!
I won't shampoo
Like every other daughter!"

So Mom says, "Fine —
You'll change your mind
And beg for soap and water!"

At first, her hair was not so bad.   But as the weeks went by,

The tangles turned to brambles

And piled up so high–

She could no longer
leave her room

No matter how she'd try.

The public health officials
Declared her room a Toxic Zone

'Cause things were living
in her hair

And some were now full-grown!

They told her that she'd have to wash

Or spend her life alone.

Claire's mom was feeling awful—

Her dad was in despair.

It seemed the little girl they loved

Was quite beyond repair~

When suddenly
their child announced,

And so,

Of course,

They found the horse,

The pizza

And the cow,

The buffalo,

The Buick,

The bird's nest

And the plough~

~And the plough~

The missing plane,

Electric train,

The llama and the goat,

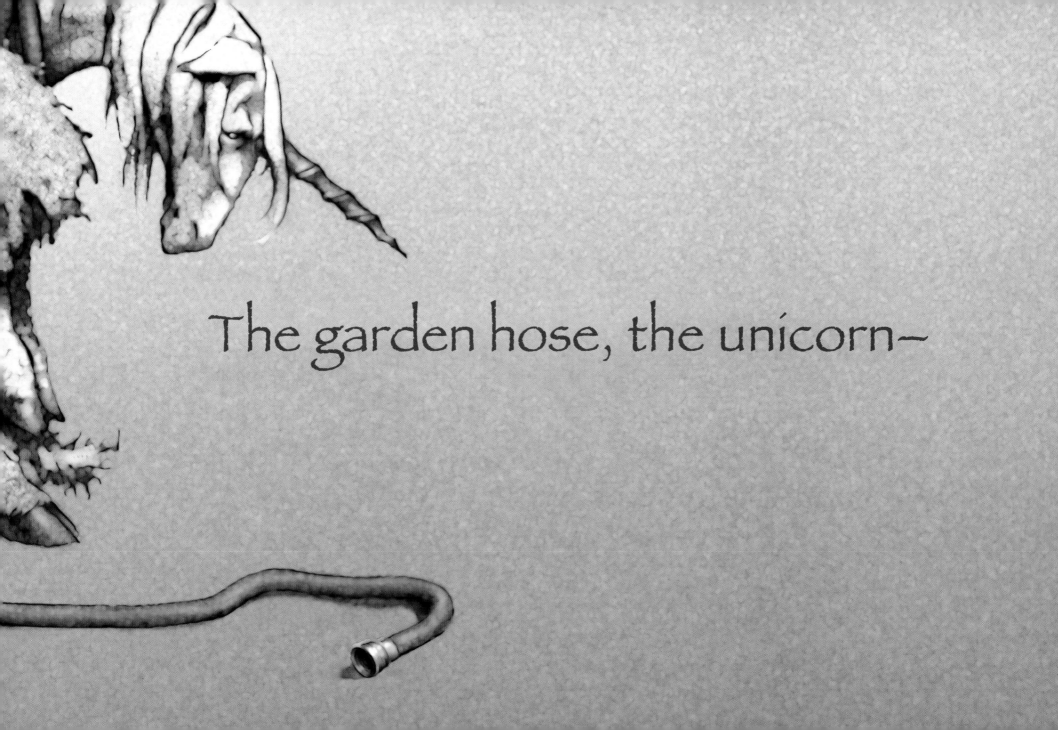

The garden hose, the unicorn~

And finally, the boat.

The house is much more pleasant now
'Cause they can breathe the air—

And Claire has
learned her lesson;
Now she likes to wash her hair.

They combed it out
and brushed it~

It looks so nice up there.

So back at school
She's looking cool
With hair that's clean and neat,

But yesterday
Claire took her bath~

And would not wash her feet!

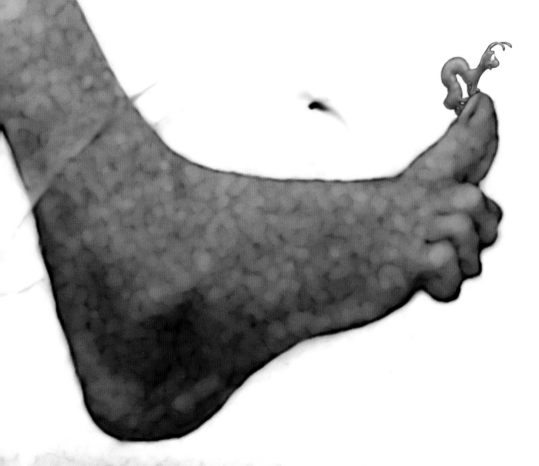